Domestic Peace

Honore de Balzac

Contents

DOMESTIC PEACE

BY

Honore de Balzac

DOMESTIC PEACE

BY
HONORE DE BALZAC

Translated By
Ellen Marriage and Clara Bell
Dedicated to my dear niece Valentine Surville.

The incident recorded in this sketch took place towards the end of the month of November, 1809, the moment when Napoleon's fugitive empire attained the apogee of its splendor. The trumpet-blasts of Wagram were still sounding an echo in the heart of the Austrian monarchy. Peace was being signed between France and the Coalition. Kings and princes came to perform their orbits, like stars, round Napoleon, who gave himself the pleasure of dragging all Europe in his train--a magnificent experiment in the power he afterwards displayed at Dresden. Never, as contemporaries tell us, did Paris see entertainments more superb than those which preceded and followed the sovereign's marriage with an Austrian archduchess. Never, in the most splendid days of the Monarchy, had so many crowned heads thronged the shores of the Seine, never had the French aristocracy been so rich or so splendid. The diamonds lavishly scattered over the women's dresses, and the gold and silver embroidery on the uniforms contrasted so strongly with the penury of the Republic, that the wealth of the globe seemed to be rolling through the drawing-rooms of Paris. Intoxication seemed to have turned the brains of this Empire of a day. All the military, not excepting their chief, reveled like parvenus in the treasure conquered for them by a million men with worsted epaulettes, whose demands were satisfied by a few yards of red ribbon.

At this time most women affected that lightness of conduct and facility of morals which distinguished the reign of Louis XV. Whether it were in imitation of the tone of the fallen monarchy, or because certain members of the Imperial family had set the example--as certain malcontents of the Faubourg Saint-Germain chose to say--it is certain that men and women alike flung themselves into a life of pleasure with an intrepidity which seemed to forbode the end of the world. But there was at that time another cause for such license. The infatuation of women for the military became a frenzy, and was too consonant to the Emperor's views for him to try to check it. The frequent calls to arms, which gave every treaty concluded between Napoleon and the rest of Europe the character of an armistice, left every passion open to a termination as sudden as the decisions of the Commander-in-chief of all these busbys, pelisses, and aiguillettes, which so fascinated the fair sex. Hearts were as nomadic as the regiments. Between the first and fifth bulletins from the /Grand Armee/ a woman might be in succession mistress, wife, mother, and widow.

Was it the prospect of early widowhood, the hope of a jointure, or that of bearing a name promised to history, which made the soldiers so attractive? Were women drawn to them by the certainty that the secret of their passions would be buried on the field of battle? or may we find the reason of this gentle fanaticism in the noble charm that courage has for a woman? Perhaps all these reasons, which the future historian of the manners of the Empire will no doubt amuse himself by weighing, counted for something in their facile readiness to abandon themselves to love intrigues. Be that as it may, it must here be confessed that at that time laurels hid many errors, women showed an ardent preference for the brave adventurers, whom they regarded as the true fount of honor, wealth, or pleasure; and in the eyes of young girls, an epaulette--the hieroglyphic of a future--signified happiness and liberty.

One feature, and a characteristic one, of this unique period in our history was an unbridled mania for everything glittering. Never were fireworks so much in vogue, never were diamonds so highly prized. The men, as greedy as the women of these translucent pebbles, displayed them no less lavishly. Possibly the necessity for carrying plunder in the most portable form made gems the fashion in the army. A man was not ridiculous then, as he would be now, if his shirt-frill or his fingers blazed with large diamonds. Murat, an Oriental by nature, set the example of preposterous luxury to modern soldiers.

The Comte de Gondreville, formerly known as Citizen Malin, whose eleva-
tion had made him famous, having become a Lucullus of the Conservative Senate,
which "conserved" nothing, had postponed an entertainment in honor of the peace
only that he might the better pay his court to Napoleon by his efforts to eclipse
those flatterers who had been before-hand with him. The ambassadors from all the
Powers friendly with France, with an eye to favors to come, the most important
personages of the Empire, and even a few princes, were at this hour assembled in
the wealthy senator's drawing-rooms. Dancing flagged; every one was watching
for the Emperor, whose presence the Count had promised his guests. And Napoleon would have kept his word but for the scene which had broken out that very
evening between him and Josephine--the scene which portended the impending
divorce of the august pair. The report of this incident, at the time kept very secret,
but recorded by history, did not reach the ears of the courtiers, and had no effect on
the gaiety of Comte de Gondreville's party beyond keeping Napoleon away.

The prettiest women in Paris, eager to be at the Count's on the strength of mere
hearsay, at this moment were a besieging force of luxury, coquettishness, elegance,
and beauty. The financial world, proud of its riches, challenged the splendor of the
generals and high officials of the Empire, so recently gorged with orders, titles, and
honors. These grand balls were always an opportunity seized upon by wealthy families for introducing their heiresses to Napoleon's Praetorian Guard, in the foolish
hope of exchanging their splendid fortunes for uncertain favors. The women who
believed themselves strong enough in their beauty alone came to test their power.
There, as elsewhere, amusement was but a blind. Calm and smiling faces and placid
brows covered sordid interests, expressions of friendship were a lie, and more than
one man was less distrustful of his enemies than of his friends.

These remarks are necessary to explain the incidents of the little imbroglio
which is the subject of this study, and the picture, softened as it is, of the tone then
dominant in Paris drawing-rooms.

"Turn your eyes a little towards the pedestal supporting that candelabrum--
do you see a young lady with her hair drawn back /a la Chinoise/!--There, in the
corner to the left; she has bluebells in the knot of chestnut curls which fall in clus-
ters on her head. Do not you see her? She is so pale you might fancy she was ill,

delicate-looking, and very small; there--now she is turning her head this way; her almond-shaped blue eyes, so delightfully soft, look as if they were made expressly for tears. Look, look! She is bending forward to see Madame de Vaudremont below the crowd of heads in constant motion; the high head-dresses prevent her having a clear view."

"I see her now, my dear fellow. You had only to say that she had the whitest skin of all the women here; I should have known whom you meant. I had noticed her before; she has the loveliest complexion I ever admired. From hence I defy you to see against her throat the pearls between the sapphires of her necklace. But she is a prude or a coquette, for the tucker of her bodice scarcely lets one suspect the beauty of her bust. What shoulders! what lily-whiteness!"

"Who is she?" asked the first speaker.

"Ah! that I do not know."

"Aristocrat!--Do you want to keep them all to yourself, Montcornet?"

"You of all men to banter me!" replied Montcornet, with a smile. "Do you think you have a right to insult a poor general like me because, being a happy rival of Soulanges, you cannot even turn on your heel without alarming Madame de Vaudremont? Or is it because I came only a month ago into the Promised Land? How insolent you can be, you men in office, who sit glued to your chairs while we are dodging shot and shell! Come, Monsieur le Maitre des Requetes, allow us to glean in the field of which you can only have precarious possession from the moment when we evacuate it. The deuce is in it! We have a right to live! My good friend, if you knew the German women, you would, I believe, do me a good turn with the Parisian you love best."

"Well, General, since you have vouchsafed to turn your attention to that lady, whom I never saw till now, have the charity to tell me if you have seen her dance."

"Why, my dear Martial, where have you dropped from? If you are ever sent with an embassy, I have small hopes of your success. Do not you see a triple rank of the most undaunted coquettes of Paris between her and the swarm of dancing men that buzz under the chandelier? And was it not only by the help of your eye-glass that you were able to discover her at all in the corner by that pillar, where she seems buried in the gloom, in spite of the candles blazing above her head? Between her and us there is such a sparkle of diamonds and glances, so many floating plumes, such a flutter of lace, of flowers and curls, that it would be a real miracle if any dancer could detect her among those stars. Why, Martial, how is it that you have not understood her to be the wife of some sous-prefet from Lippe or Dyle, who has come to try to get her husband promoted?"

"Oh, he will be!" exclaimed the Master of Appeals quickly.

"I doubt it," replied the Colonel of Cuirassiers, laughing. "She seems as raw in intrigue as you are in diplomacy. I dare bet, Martial, that you do not know how she got into that place."

The lawyer looked at the Colonel of Cuirassiers with an expression as much of contempt as of curiosity.

"Well," proceeded Montcornet, "she arrived, I have no doubt, punctually at nine, the first of the company perhaps, and probably she greatly embarrassed the Comtesse de Gondreville, who cannot put two ideas together. Repulsed by the mistress of the house, routed from chair to chair by each newcomer, and driven into the darkness of this little corner, she allowed herself to be walled in, the victim of the jealousy of the other ladies, who would gladly have buried that dangerous beauty. She had, of course, no friend to encourage her to maintain the place she first held in the front rank; then each of those treacherous fair ones would have enjoined on the men of her circle on no account to take out our poor friend, under pain of the severest punishment. That, my dear fellow, is the way in which those sweet faces, in appearance so tender and so artless, would have formed a coalition against the stranger, and that without a word beyond the question, 'Tell me, dear, do you know that little woman in blue?' --Look here, Martial, if you care to run the gauntlet of more flattering glances and inviting questions than you will ever again meet in the whole of your life, just try to get through the triple rampart which defends that Queen of Dyle, or Lippe, or Charente. You will see whether the dullest woman of them all will not be equal to inventing some wile that would hinder the most determined man from bringing the plaintive stranger to the light. Does it not strike you that she looks like an elegy?"

"Do you think so, Montcornet? Then she must be a married woman?"

"Why not a widow?"

"She would be less passive," said the lawyer, laughing.

"She is perhaps the widow of a man who is gambling," replied the handsome Colonel.

"To be sure; since the peace there are so many widows of that class!" said Martial. "But my dear Montcornet, we are a couple of simpletons. That face is still too ingenuous, there is too much youth and freshness on the brow and temples for her to be married. What splendid flesh-tints! Nothing has sunk in the modeling of the nose. Lips, chin, everything in her face is as fresh as a white rosebud, though the expression is veiled, as it were, by the clouds of sadness. Who can it be that makes that young creature weep?"

"Women cry for so little," said the Colonel.

"I do not know," replied Martial; "but she does not cry because she is left there without a partner; her grief is not of to-day. It is evident that she has beautified herself for this evening with intention. I would wager that she is in love already."

"Bah! She is perhaps the daughter of some German princeling; no one talks to her," said Montcornet.

"Dear! how unhappy a poor child may be!" Martial went on. "Can there be anything more graceful and refined than our little stranger? Well, not one of those furies who stand round her, and who believe that they can feel, will say a word to her. If she would but speak, we should see if she has fine teeth."

"Bless me, you boil over like milk at the least increase of temperature!" cried the Colonel, a little nettled at so soon finding a rival in his friend.

"What!" exclaimed the lawyer, without heeding the Colonel's question. "Can nobody here tell us the name of this exotic flower?"

"Some lady companion!" said Montcornet.

"What next? A companion! wearing sapphires fit for a queen, and a dress of Malines lace? Tell that to the marines, General. You, too, would not shine in diplomacy if, in the course of your conjectures, you jump in a breath from a German princess to a lady companion."

Montcornet stopped a man by taking his arm--a fat little man, whose iron-gray hair and clever eyes were to be seen at the lintel of every doorway, and who mingled unceremoniously with the various groups which welcomed him respectfully.

"Gondreville, my friend," said Montcornet, "who is that quite charming little woman sitting out there under that huge candelabrum?"

"The candelabrum? Ravrio's work; Isabey made the design."

"Oh, I recognized your lavishness and taste; but the lady?"

"Ah! I do not know. Some friend of my wife's, no doubt."

"Or your mistress, you old rascal."

"No, on my honor. The Comtesse de Gondreville is the only person capable of inviting people whom no one knows."

In spite of this very acrimonious comment, the fat little man's lips did not lose the smile which the Colonel's suggestion had brought to them. Montcornet returned to the lawyer, who had rejoined a neighboring group, intent on asking, but in vain, for information as to the fair unknown. He grasped Martial's arm, and said in his ear:

"My dear Martial, mind what you are about. Madame de Vaudremont has been watching you for some minutes with ominous attentiveness; she is a woman who can guess by the mere movement of your lips what you say to me; our eyes have already told her too much; she has perceived and followed their direction, and I suspect that at this moment she is thinking even more than we are of the little blue lady."

"That is too old a trick in warfare, my dear Montcornet! However, what do I care? Like the Emperor, when I have made a conquest, I keep it."

"Martial, your fatuity cries out for a lesson. What! you, a civilian, and so lucky as to be the husband-designate of Madame de Vaudremont, a widow of two-and-twenty, burdened with four thousand napoleons a year --a woman who slips such a diamond as this on your finger," he added, taking the lawyer's left hand, which the young man complacently allowed; "and, to crown all, you affect the Lovelace, just as if you were a colonel and obliged to keep up the reputation of the military in home quarters! Fie, fie! Only think of all you may lose."

"At any rate, I shall not lose my liberty," replied Martial, with a forced laugh.

He cast a passionate glance at Madame de Vaudremont, who responded only by a smile of some uneasiness, for she had seen the Colonel examining the lawyer's ring.

"Listen to me, Martial. If you flutter round my young stranger, I shall set to work to win Madame de Vaudremont."

"You have my full permission, my dear Cuirassier, but you will not gain this much," and the young Maitre des Requetes put his polished thumb-nail under an upper tooth with a little mocking click.

"Remember that I am unmarried," said the Colonel; "that my sword is my whole fortune; and that such a challenge is setting Tantalus down to a banquet which he will devour."

"Prrr."

This defiant roll of consonants was the only reply to the Colonel's declaration, as Martial looked him from head to foot before turning away.

The fashion of the time required men to wear at a ball white kerseymere breeches and silk stockings. This pretty costume showed to great advantage the perfection of Montcornet's fine shape. He was five-and-thirty, and attracted attention by his stalwart height, insisted on for the Cuirassiers of the Imperial Guard whose handsome uniform enhanced the dignity of his figure, still youthful in spite of the stoutness occasioned by living on horseback. A black moustache emphasized the frank expression of a thoroughly soldierly countenance, with a broad, high forehead, an aquiline nose, and bright red lips. Montcornet's manner, stamped with a certain superiority due to the habit of command, might please a woman sensible enough not to aim at making a slave of her husband. The Colonel smiled as he looked at the lawyer, one of his favorite college friends, whose small figure made it necessary for Montcornet to look down a little as he answered his raillery with a friendly glance.

Baron Martial de la Roche-Hugon was a young Provencal patronized by Napoleon; his fate might probably be some splendid embassy. He had won the Emperor by his Italian suppleness and a genius for intrigue, a drawing-room eloquence, and a knowledge of manners, which are so good a substitute for the higher qualities of a sterling man. Through young and eager, his face had already acquired the rigid brilliancy of tinned iron, one of the indispensable characteristics of diplomatists, which allows them to conceal their emotions and disguise their feelings, unless, indeed, this impassibility indicates an absence of all emotion and the death of every feeling. The heart of a diplomate may be regarded as an insoluble problem, for the three most illustrious ambassadors of the time have been distinguished by perdurable hatreds and most romantic attachments.

Martial, however, was one of those men who are capable of reckoning on the future in the midst of their intensest enjoyment; he had already learned to judge the world, and hid his ambition under the fatuity of a lady-killer, cloaking his talent under the commonplace of mediocrity as soon as he observed the rapid advancement of those men who gave the master little umbrage.

The two friends now had to part with a cordial grasp of hands. The introductory tune, warning the ladies to form in squares for a fresh quadrille, cleared the men away from the space they had filled while talking in the middle of the large room. This hurried dialogue had taken place during the usual interval between two dances, in front of the fireplace of the great drawing-room of Gondreville's mansion. The questions and answers of this very ordinary ballroom gossip had been almost whispered by each of the speakers into his neighbor's ear. At the same time, the chandeliers and the flambeaux on the chimney-shelf shed such a flood of light on the two friends that their faces, strongly illuminated, failed, in spite of their diplomatic discretion, to conceal the faint expression of their feelings either from the keen-sighted countess or the artless stranger. This espionage of people's thoughts is perhaps to idle persons one of the pleasures they find in society, while numbers of disappointed numskulls are bored there without daring to own it.

Fully to appreciate the interest of this conversation, it is necessary to relate an incident which would presently serve as an invisible bond, drawing together the actors in this little drama, who were at present scattered through the rooms.

At about eleven o'clock, just as the dancers were returning to their seats, the company had observed the entrance of the handsomest woman in Paris, the queen of fashion, the only person wanting to the brilliant assembly. She made it a rule never to appear till the moment when a party had reached that pitch of excited movement which does not allow the women to preserve much longer the freshness of their faces or of their dress. This brief hour is, as it were, the springtime of a ball. An hour after, when pleasure falls flat and fatigue is encroaching, everything is spoilt. Madame de Vaudremont never committed the blunder of remaining at a party to be seen with drooping flowers, hair out of curl, tumbled frills, and a face like every other that sleep is courting--not always without success. She took good care not to let her beauty be seen drowsy, as her rivals did; she was so clever as to keep up her reputation for smartness by always leaving a ballroom in brilliant order, as she had entered it. Women whispered to each other with a feeling of envy that she planned and wore as many different dresses as the parties she went to in one evening.

On the present occasion Madame de Vaudremont was not destined to be free to leave when she would the ballroom she had entered in triumph. Pausing for a moment on the threshold, she shot swift but observant glances on the women present, hastily scrutinizing their dresses to assure herself that her own eclipsed them all.

The illustrious beauty presented herself to the admiration of the crowd at the same moment with one of the bravest colonels of the Guards' Artillery and the Emperor's favorite, the Comte de Soulanges. The transient and fortuitous association of these two had about it a certain air of mystery. On hearing the names announced of Monsieur de Soulanges and the Comtesse de Vaudremont, a few women sitting by the wall rose, and men, hurrying in from the side-rooms, pressed forward to the principal doorway. One of the jesters who are always to be found in any large assembly said, as the Countess and her escort came in, that "women had quite as much curiosity about seeing a man who was faithful to his passion as men had in studying a woman who was difficult to enthrall."

Though the Comte de Soulanges, a young man of about two-and-thirty, was endowed with the nervous temperament which in a man gives rise to fine qualities, his slender build and pale complexion were not at first sight attractive; his black eyes betrayed great vivacity, but he was taciturn in company, and there was nothing in his appearance to reveal the gift for oratory which subsequently distinguished him, on the Right, in the legislative assembly under the Restoration.

The Comtesse de Vaudremont, a tall woman, rather fat, with a skin of dazzling whiteness, a small head that she carried well, and the immense advantage of inspiring love by the graciousness of her manner, was one of those beings who keep all the promise of their beauty.

The pair, who for a few minutes were the centre of general observation, did not for long give curiosity an opportunity of exercising itself about them. The Colonel and the Countess seemed perfectly to understand that accident had placed them in an awkward position. Martial, as they came forward, had hastened to join the group of men by the fireplace, that he might watch Madame de Vaudremont with the jealous anxiety of the first flame of passion, from behind the heads which formed a sort of rampart; a secret voice seemed to warn him that the success on which he prided himself might perhaps be precarious. But the coldly polite smile with which the Countess thanked Monsieur de Soulanges, and her little bow of dismissal as she sat down by Madame de Gondreville, relaxed the muscles of his face which jealousy had made rigid. Seeing Soulanges, however, still standing quite near the sofa on which Madame de Vaudremont was seated, not apparently having understood the glance by which the lady had conveyed to him that they were both playing a ridiculous part, the volcanic Provencal again knit the black brows that overshadowed his blue eyes, smoothed his chestnut curls to keep himself in countenance, and without betraying the agitation which made his heart beat, watched the faces of the Countess and of M. de Soulanges while still chatting with his neighbors. He then took the hand of Colonel Montcornet, who had just renewed their old acquaintance, but he listened to him without hearing him; his mind was elsewhere.

Soulanges was gazing calmly at the women, sitting four ranks deep all round the immense ballroom, admiring this dado of diamonds, rubies, masses of gold and shining hair, of which the lustre almost outshone the blaze of waxlights, the cut-glass of the chandeliers, and the gilding. His rival's stolid indifference put the lawyer out of countenance. Quite incapable of controlling his secret transports of impatience, Martial went towards Madame de Vaudremont with a bow. On seeing the Provencal, Soulanges gave him a covert glance, and impertinently turned away his head. Solemn silence now reigned in the room, where curiosity was at the highest pitch. All these eager faces wore the strangest mixed expressions; every one apprehended one of those outbreaks which men of breeding carefully avoid. Suddenly the Count's pale face turned as red as the scarlet facings of his coat, and he fixed his gaze on the floor that the cause of his agitation might not be guessed. On catching sight of the unknown lady humbly seated by the pedestal of the candelabrum, he moved away with a melancholy air, passing in front of the lawyer, and took refuge in one of the cardrooms. Martial and all the company thought that Soulanges had publicly surrendered the post, out of fear of the ridicule which invariably attaches to a discarded lover. The lawyer proudly raised his head and looked at the strange lady; then, as he took his seat at his ease near Madame de Vaudremont, he listened to her so inattentively that he did not catch these words spoken behind her fan:

"Martial, you will oblige me this evening by not wearing that ring that you snatched from me. I have my reasons, and will explain them to you in a moment

when we go away. You must give me your arm to go to the Princess de Wagram's."

"Why did you come in with the Colonel?" asked the Baron.

"I met him in the hall," she replied. "But leave me now; everybody is looking
at us."

Martial returned to the Colonel of Cuirassiers. Then it was that the little blue
lady had become the object of the curiosity which agitated in such various ways the
Colonel, Soulanges, Martial, and Madame de Vaudremont.

When the friends parted, after the challenge which closed their conversation,
the Baron flew to Madame de Vaudremont, and led her to a place in the most brilliant quadrille. Favored by the sort of intoxication which dancing always produces
in a woman, and by the turmoil of a ball, where men appear in all the trickery of
dress, which adds no less to their attractions than it does to those of women, Martial thought he might yield with impunity to the charm that attracted his gaze to
the fair stranger. Though he succeeded in hiding his first glances towards the lady
in blue from the anxious activity of the Countess' eyes, he was ere long caught in
the fact; and though he managed to excuse himself once for his absence of mind,
he could not justify the unseemly silence with which he presently heard the most
insinuating question which a woman can put to a man:

"Do you like me very much this evening?"

And the more dreamy he became, the more the Countess pressed and teased
him.

While Martial was dancing, the Colonel moved from group to group, seeking
information about the unknown lady. After exhausting the good-humor even of the
most indifferent, he had resolved to take advantage of a moment when the Comtesse
de Gondreville seemed to be at liberty, to ask her the name of the mysterious lady,
when he perceived a little space left clear between the pedestal of the candelabrum
and the two sofas, which ended in that corner. The dance had left several of the
chairs vacant, which formed rows of fortifications held by mothers or women of
middle age; and the Colonel seized the opportunity to make his way through this
palisade hung with shawls and wraps. He began by making himself agreeable to the
dowagers, and so from one to another, and from compliment to compliment, he
at last reached the empty space next the stranger. At the risk of catching on to the

gryphons and chimaeras of the huge candelabrum, he stood there, braving the glare and dropping of the wax candles, to Martial's extreme annoyance.

The Colonel, far too tactful to speak suddenly to the little blue lady on his right, began by saying to a plain woman who was seated on the left:

"This is a splendid ball, madame! What luxury! What life! On my word, every woman here is pretty! You are not dancing--because you do not care for it, no doubt."

This vapid conversation was solely intended to induce his right-hand neighbor to speak; but she, silent and absent-minded, paid not the least attention. The officer had in store a number of phrases which he intended should lead up to: "And you, madame?"--a question from which he hoped great things. But he was strangely surprised to see tears in the strange lady's eyes, which seemed wholly absorbed in gazing on Madame de Vaudremont.

"You are married, no doubt, madame?" he asked her at length, in hesitating tones.

"Yes, monsieur," replied the lady.

"And your husband is here, of course?"

"Yes, monsieur."

"And why, madame, do you remain in this spot? Is it to attract attention?"

The mournful lady smiled sadly.

"Allow me the honor, madame, of being your partner in the next quadrille, and I will take care not to bring you back here. I see a vacant settee near the fire; come and take it. When so many people are ready to ascend the throne, and Royalty is the mania of the day, I cannot imagine that you will refuse the title of Queen of the Ball which your beauty may claim."

"I do not intend to dance, monsieur."

The curt tone of the lady's replies was so discouraging that the Colonel found himself compelled to raise the siege. Martial, who guessed what the officer's last request had been, and the refusal he had met with, began to smile, and stroked his chin, making the diamond sparkle which he wore on his finger.

"What are you laughing at?" said the Comtesse de Vaudremont.

"At the failure of the poor Colonel, who has just put his foot in it----"

"I begged you to take your ring off," said the Countess, interrupting him.

"I did not hear you."

"If you can hear nothing this evening, at any rate you see everything, Monsieur le Baron," said Madame de Vaudremont, with an air of vexation.

"That young man is displaying a very fine diamond," the stranger remarked to the Colonel.

"Splendid," he replied. "The man is the Baron Martial de la Roche-Hugon, one of my most intimate friends."

"I have to thank you for telling me his name," she went on; "he seems an agreeable man."

"Yes, but he is rather fickle."

"He seems to be on the best terms with the Comtesse de Vaudremont?" said the lady, with an inquiring look at the Colonel.

"On the very best."

The unknown turned pale.

"Hallo!" thought the soldier, "she is in love with that lucky devil Martial."

"I fancied that Madame de Vaudremont had long been devoted to M. de Soulanges," said the lady, recovering a little from the suppressed grief which had clouded the fairness of her face.

"For a week past the Countess has been faithless," replied the Colonel. "But you must have seen poor Soulanges when he came in; he is till trying to disbelieve in his disaster."

"Yes, I saw him," said the lady. Then she added, "Thank you very much, monsieur," in a tone which signified a dismissal.

At this moment the quadrille was coming to an end. Montcornet had only time to withdraw, saying to himself by way of consolation, "She is married."

"Well, valiant Cuirassier," exclaimed the Baron, drawing the Colonel aside into a window-bay to breathe the fresh air from the garden, "how are you getting on?"

"She is a married woman, my dear fellow."

"What does that matter?"

"Oh, deuce take it! I am a decent sort of man," replied the Colonel. "I have no idea of paying my addresses to a woman I cannot marry. Besides, Martial, she expressly told me that she did not intend to dance."

"Colonel, I will bet a hundred napoleons to your gray horse that she will dance with me this evening."

"Done!" said the Colonel, putting his hand in the coxcomb's. "Meanwhile I am going to look for Soulanges; he perhaps knows the lady, as she seems interested in him."

"You have lost, my good fellow," cried Martial, laughing. "My eyes have met hers, and I know what they mean. My dear friend, you owe me no grudge for dancing with her after she has refused you?"

"No, no. Those who laugh last, laugh longest. But I am an honest gambler and a generous enemy, Martial, and I warn you, she is fond of diamonds."

With these words the friends parted; General Montcornet made his way to the cardroom, where he saw the Comte de Soulanges sitting at a /bouillotte/ table. Though there was no friendship between the two soldiers, beyond the superficial comradeship arising from the perils of war and the duties of the service, the Colonel of Cuirassiers was painfully struck by seeing the Colonel of Artillery, whom he knew to be a prudent man, playing at a game which might bring him to ruin. The heaps of gold and notes piled on the fateful cards showed the frenzy of play. A circle of silent men stood round the players at the table. Now and then a few words were spoken--/pass, play, I stop, a thousand Louis, taken/--but, looking at the five motionless men, it seemed as though they talked only with their eyes. As the Colonel, alarmed by Soulanges' pallor, went up to him, the Count was winning. Field-Marshal the Duc d'Isemberg, Keller, and a famous banker rose from the table completely cleaned out of considerable sums. Soulanges looked gloomier than ever as he swept up a quantity of gold and notes; he did not even count it; his lips curled with bitter scorn, he seemed to defy fortune rather than be grateful for her favors.

"Courage," said the Colonel. "Courage, Soulanges!" Then, believing he would do him a service by dragging him from play, he added: "Come with me. I have some good news for you, but on one condition."

"What is that?" asked Soulanges.

"That you will answer a question I will ask you."

The Comte de Soulanges rose abruptly, placing his winnings with reckless indifference in his handkerchief, which he had been twisting with convulsive nervousness, and his expression was so savage that none of the players took exception to his walking off with their money. Indeed, every face seemed to dilate with relief when his morose and crabbed countenance was no longer to be seen under the circle of light which a shaded lamp casts on a gaming-table.

"Those fiends of soldiers are always as thick as thieves at a fair!" said a diplomate who had been looking on, as he took Soulanges' place. One single pallid and fatigued face turned to the newcomer, and said with a glance that flashed and died out like the sparkle of a diamond: "When we say military men, we do not mean civil, Monsieur le Ministre."

"My dear fellow," said Montcornet to Soulanges, leading him into a corner, "the Emperor spoke warmly in your praise this morning, and your promotion to be field-marshal is a certainty."

"The Master does not love the Artillery."

"No, but he adores the nobility, and you are an aristocrat. The Master said," added Montcornet, "that the men who had married in Paris during the campaign were not therefore to be considered in disgrace. Well then?"

The Comte de Soulanges looked as if he understood nothing of this speech.

"And now I hope," the Colonel went on, "that you will tell me if you know a charming little woman who is sitting under a huge candelabrum----"

At these words the Count's face lighted up; he violently seized the Colonel's hand: "My dear General," said he, in a perceptibly altered voice, "if any man but you had asked me such a question, I would have cracked his skull with this mass of gold. Leave me, I entreat you. I feel more like blowing out my brains this evening, I assure you, than ----I hate everything I see. And, in fact, I am going. This gaiety, this music, these stupid faces, all laughing, are killing me!"

"My poor friend!" replied Montcornet gently, and giving the Count's hand a friendly pressure, "you are too vehement. What would you say if I told you that Martial is thinking so little of Madame de Vaudremont that he is quite smitten with that little lady?"

"If he says a word to her," cried Soulanges, stammering with rage, "I will thrash him as flat as his own portfolio, even if the coxcomb were in the Emperor's lap!"

And he sank quite overcome on an easy-chair to which Montcornet had led him. The colonel slowly went away, for he perceived that Soulanges was in a state of fury far too violent for the pleasantries or the attentions of superficial friendship to soothe him.

When Montcornet returned to the ballroom, Madame de Vaudremont was the first person on whom his eyes fell, and he observed on her face, usually so calm, some symptoms of ill-disguised agitation. A chair was vacant near hers, and the Colonel seated himself.

"I dare wager something has vexed you?" said he.

"A mere trifle, General. I want to be gone, for I have promised to go to a ball at the Grand Duchess of Berg's, and I must look in first at the Princesse de Wagram's. Monsieur de la Roche-Hugon, who knows this, is amusing himself by flirting with the dowagers."

"That is not the whole secret of your disturbance, and I will bet a hundred louis that you will remain here the whole evening."

"Impertinent man!"

"Then I have hit the truth?"

"Well, tell me, what am I thinking of?" said the Countess, tapping the Colonel's fingers with her fan. "I might even reward you if you guess rightly."

"I will not accept the challenge; I have too much the advantage of you."

"You are presumptuous."

"You are afraid of seeing Martial at the feet----"

"Of whom?" cried the Countess, affecting surprise.

"Of that candelabrum," replied the Colonel, glancing at the fair stranger, and then looking at the Countess with embarrassing scrutiny.

"You have guessed it," replied the coquette, hiding her face behind her fan, which she began to play with. "Old Madame de Lansac, who is, you know, as malicious as an old monkey," she went on, after a pause, "has just told me that Monsieur de la Roche-Hugon is running into danger by flirting with that stranger, who sits here this evening like a skeleton at a feast. I would rather see a death's head than that face, so cruelly beautiful, and as pale as a ghost. She is my evil genius.--Madame de Lansac," she added, after a flash and gesture of annoyance, "who only goes to a ball to watch everything while pretending to sleep, has made me miserably anxious. Martial shall pay dearly for playing me such a trick. Urge him, meanwhile, since he is your friend, not to make me so unhappy."

"I have just been with a man who promises to blow his brains out, and nothing less, if he speaks to that little lady. And he is a man, madame, to keep his word. But then I know Martial; such threats are to him an encouragement. And, besides, we have wagered----" Here the Colonel lowered his voice.

"Can it be true?" said the Countess.

"On my word of honor."

"Thank you, my dear Colonel," replied Madame de Vaudremont, with a glance full of invitation.

"Will you do me the honor of dancing with me?"

"Yes; but the next quadrille. During this one I want to find out what will come of this little intrigue, and to ascertain who the little blue lady may be; she looks intelligent."

The Colonel, understanding that Madame de Vaudremont wished to be alone, retired, well content to have begun his attack so well.

At most entertainments women are to be met who are there, like Madame de Lansac, as old sailors gather on the seashore to watch younger mariners struggling with the tempest. At this moment Madame de Lansac, who seemed to be interested in the personages of this drama, could easily guess the agitation which the Countess was going through. The lady might fan herself gracefully, smile on the young men who bowed to her, and bring into play all the arts by which a woman hides her emotion,--the Dowager, one of the most clear-sighted and mischief-loving duchesses bequeathed by the eighteenth century to the nineteenth, could read her heart and mind through it all.

The old lady seemed to detect the slightest movement that revealed the impressions of the soul. The imperceptible frown that furrowed that calm, pure forehead, the faintest quiver of the cheeks, the curve of the eyebrows, the least curl of the lips, whose living coral could conceal nothing from her,--all these were to the Duchess like the print of a book. From the depths of her large arm-chair, completely filled by the flow of her dress, the coquette of the past, while talking to a diplomate who had sought her out to hear the anecdotes she told so cleverly, was admiring herself in the younger coquette; she felt kindly to her, seeing how bravely she disguised her annoyance and grief of heart. Madame de Vaudremont, in fact, felt as much sorrow as she feigned cheerfulness; she had believed that she had found in Martial a man of talent on whose support she could count for adorning her life with all the enchantment of power; and at this moment she perceived her mistake, as injurious to her reputation as to her good opinion of herself. In her, as in other women of that time, the suddenness of their passions increased their vehemence. Souls which love much and love often, suffer no less than those which burn themselves out in one affection. Her liking for Martial was but of yesterday, it is true, but the least experienced surgeon knows that the pain caused by the amputation of a healthy limb is more acute than the removal of a diseased one. There was a future before Madame de Vaudremont's passion for Martial, while her previous love had been hopeless, and poisoned by Soulanges' remorse.

The old Duchess, who was watching for an opportunity of speaking to the Countess, hastened to dismiss her Ambassador; for in comparison with a lover's quarrel every interest pales, even with an old woman. To engage battle, Madame de Lansac shot at the younger lady a sardonic glance which made the Countess fear lest her fate was in the dowager's hands. There are looks between woman and woman which are like the torches brought on at the climax of a tragedy. No one who had not known that Duchess could appreciate the terror which the expression of her countenance inspired in the Countess.

Madame de Lansac was tall, and her features led people to say, "That must have been a handsome woman!" She coated her cheeks so thickly with rouge that the wrinkles were scarcely visible; but her eyes, far from gaining a factitious brilliancy from this strong carmine, looked all the more dim. She wore a vast quantity of diamonds, and dressed with sufficient taste not to make herself ridiculous. Her sharp nose promised epigram. A well-fitted set of teeth preserved a smile of such irony as recalled that of Voltaire. At the same time, the exquisite politeness of her manners so effectually softened the mischievous twist in her mind, that it was impossible to accuse her of spitefulness.

The old woman's eyes lighted up, and a triumphant glance, seconded by a smile, which said, "I promised you as much!" shot across the room, and brought a blush of hope to the pale cheeks of the young creature languishing under the great chandelier. The alliance between Madame de Lansac and the stranger could not escape the practised eye of the Comtesse de Vaudremont, who scented a mystery, and was determined to penetrate it.

At this instant the Baron de la Roche-Hugon, after questioning all the dowagers without success as to the blue lady's name, applied in despair to the Comtesse de

Gondreville, from whom he reached only this unsatisfactory reply, "A lady whom the 'ancient' Duchesse de Lansac introduced to me."

Turning by chance towards the armchair occupied by the old lady, the lawyer intercepted the glance of intelligence she sent to the stranger; and although he had for some time been on bad terms with her, he determined to speak to her. The "ancient" Duchess, seeing the jaunty Baron prowling round her chair, smiled with sardonic irony, and looked at Madame de Vaudremont with an expression that made Montcornet laugh.

"If the old witch affects to be friendly," thought the Baron, "she is certainly going to play me some spiteful trick.--Madame," he said, "you have, I am told, undertaken the charge of a very precious treasure."

"Do you take me for a dragon?" said the old lady. "But of whom are you speaking?" she added, with a sweetness which revived Martial's hopes.

"Of that little lady, unknown to all, whom the jealousy of all these coquettes has imprisoned in that corner. You, no doubt, know her family?"

"Yes," said the Duchess. "But what concern have you with a provincial heiress, married some time since, a woman of good birth, whom you none of you know, you men; she goes nowhere."

"Why does not she dance, she is such a pretty creature?--May we conclude a treaty of peace? If you will vouchsafe to tell me all I want to know, I promise you that a petition for the restitution of the woods of Navarreins by the Commissioners of Crown Lands shall be strongly urged on the Emperor."

The younger branch of the house of Navarreins bears quarterly with the arms of Navarreins those of Lansac, namely, azure, and argent party per pale raguly, between six spear-heads in pale, and the old lady's liaison with Louis XV. had earned her husband the title of duke by royal patent. Now, as the Navarreins had not yet resettled in France, it was sheer trickery that the young lawyer thus proposed to the old lady by suggesting to her that she should petition for an estate belonging to the elder branch of the family.

"Monsieur," said the old woman with deceptive gravity, "bring the Comtesse de Vaudremont across to me. I promise you that I will reveal to her the mystery of the interesting unknown. You see, every man in the room has reached as great a curiosity as your own. All eyes are involuntarily turned towards the corner where my protegee has so modestly placed herself; she is reaping all the homage the women wished to deprive her of. Happy the man she chooses for her partner!" She interrupted herself, fixing her eyes on Madame de Vaudremont with one of those looks which plainly say, "We are talking of you."--Then she added, "I imagine you would rather learn the stranger's name from the lips of your handsome Countess than from mine."

There was such marked defiance in the Duchess' attitude that Madame de Vaudremont rose, came up to her, and took the chair Martial placed for her; then without noticing him she said, "I can guess, madame, that you are talking of me; but I admit my want of perspicacity; I do not know whether it is for good or evil."

Madame de Lansac pressed the young woman's pretty hand in her own dry and wrinkled fingers, and answered in a low, compassionate tone, "Poor child!"

The women looked at each other. Madame de Vaudremont understood that Martial was in the way, and dismissed him, saying with an imperious expression, "Leave us."

The Baron, ill-pleased at seeing the Countess under the spell of the dangerous sibyl who had drawn her to her side gave one of those looks which a man can give-potent over a blinded heart, but simply ridiculous in the eyes of a woman who is beginning to criticise the man who has attracted her.

"Do you think you can play the Emperor?" said Madame de Vaudremont, turning three-quarters of her face to fix an ironical sidelong gaze on the lawyer.

Martial was too much a man of the world, and had too much wit and acumen, to risk breaking with a woman who was in favor at Court, and whom the Emperor wished to see married. He counted, too, on the jealousy he intended to provoke in her as the surest means of discovering the secret of her coolness, and withdrew all the more willingly, because at this moment a new quadrille was putting everybody in motion.

With an air of making room for the dancing, the Baron leaned back against the marble slab of a console, folded his arms, and stood absorbed in watching the two ladies talking. From time to time he followed the glances which both frequently directed to the stranger. Then, comparing the Countess with the new beauty, made so attractive by a touch of mystery, the Baron fell a prey to the detestable self-interest common to adventurous lady-killers; he hesitated between a fortune within his grasp and the indulgence of his caprice. The blaze of light gave such strong relief to his anxious and sullen face, against the hangings of white silk moreen brushed by his black hair, that he might have been compared to an evil genius. Even from a distance more than one observer no doubt said to himself, "There is another poor wretch who seems to be enjoying himself!"

The Colonel, meanwhile, with one shoulder leaning lightly against the side-post of the doorway between the ballroom and the cardroom, could laugh undetected under his ample moustache; it amused him to look on at the turmoil of the dance; he could see a hundred pretty heads turning about in obedience to the figures; he could read in some faces, as in those of the Countess and his friend Martial, the secrets of their agitation; and then, looking round, he wondered what connection there could be between the gloomy looks of the Comte de Soulanges, still seated on the sofa, and the plaintive expression of the fair unknown, on whose features the joys of hope and the anguish of involuntary dread were alternately legible. Montcornet stood like the king of the feast. In this moving picture he saw a complete presentment of the world, and he laughed at it as he found himself the object of inviting smiles from a hundred beautiful and elegant women. A Colonel of the Imperial Guard, a position equal to that of a Brigadier-General, was undoubtedly one of the best matches in the army.

It was now nearly midnight. The conversation, the gambling, the dancing, the flirtations, interests, petty rivalries, and scheming had all reached the pitch of ardor which makes a young man exclaim involuntarily, "A fine ball!"

"My sweet little angel," said Madame de Lansac to the Countess, "you are now at an age when in my day I made many mistakes. Seeing you are just now enduring a thousand deaths, it occurred to me that I might give you some charitable advice. To go wrong at two-and-twenty means spoiling your future; is it not tearing the gown you must wear? My dear, it is not much later that we learn to go about in it without crumpling it. Go on, sweetheart, making clever enemies, and friends who have no sense of conduct, and you will see what a pleasant life you will some day be leading!"

"Oh, madame, it is very hard for a woman to be happy, do not you think?" the Countess eagerly exclaimed.

"My child, at your age you must learn to choose between pleasure and happiness. You want to marry Martial, who is not fool enough to make a good husband, nor passionate enough to remain a lover. He is in debt, my dear; he is the man to run through your fortune; still, that would be nothing if he could make you happy.--Do not you see how aged he is? The man must have been ill; he is making the most of what is left him. In three years he will be a wreck. Then he will be ambitious; perhaps he may succeed. I do not think so.--What is he? A man of intrigue, who may have the business faculty to perfection, and be able to gossip agreeably; but he is too presumptuous to have any sterling merit; he will not go far. Besides--only look at him. Is it not written on his brow that, at this very moment, what he sees in you is not a young and pretty woman, but the two million francs you possess? He does not love you, my dear; he is reckoning you up as if you were an investment. If you are bent on marrying, find an older man who has an assured position and is half-way on his career. A widow's marriage ought not to be a trivial love affair. Is a mouse to be caught a second time in the same trap? A new alliance ought now to be a good speculation on your part, and in marrying again you ought at least to have a hope of being some day addressed as Madame la Marechale!"

As she spoke, both women naturally fixed their eyes on Colonel Montcornet's handsome face.

"If you would rather play the delicate part of a flirt and not marry again," the Duchess went on, with blunt good-nature; "well! my poor child, you, better than any woman, will know how to raise the storm-clouds and disperse them again. But, I beseech you, never make it your pleasure to disturb the peace of families, to destroy unions, and ruin the happiness of happy wives. I, my dear, have played that perilous game. Dear heaven! for a triumph of vanity some poor virtuous soul is murdered-- for there really are virtuous women, child,--and we may make ourselves mortally hated. I learned, a little too late, that, as the Duc d'Albe once said, one salmon is worth a thousand frogs! A genuine affection certainly brings a thousand times more happiness than the transient passions we may inspire.--Well, I came here on purpose to preach to you; yes, you are the cause of my appearance in this house, which stinks of the lower class. Have I not just seen actors here? Formerly, my dear, we received them in our boudoir; but in the drawing-room--never!--Why do you look at me with so much amazement? Listen to me. If you want to play with men, do not try to wring the hearts of any but those whose life is not yet settled, who have no duties to fulfil; the others do not forgive us for the errors that have made them happy. Profit by this maxim, founded on my long experience.--That luckless Soulanges, for instance, whose head you have turned, whom you have intoxicated for these fifteen months past, God knows how! Do you know at what you have struck?--At his whole life. He has been married these two years; he is worshiped by a charming wife, whom he loves, but neglects; she lives in tears and embittered silence. Soulanges has had hours of remorse more terrible than his pleasure has been sweet. And you, you artful little thing, have deserted him.--Well, come and see your work."

The old lady took Madame de Vaudremont's hand, and they rose.

"There," said Madame de Lansac, and her eyes showed her the stranger, sitting pale and tremulous under the glare of the candles, "that is my grandniece, the Comtesse de Soulanges; to-day she yielded at last to my persuasion, and consented to leave the sorrowful room, where the sight of her child gives her but little consolation. You see her? You think her charming? Then imagine, dear Beauty, what she must have been when happiness and love shed their glory on that face now blighted."

The Countess looked away in silence, and seemed lost in sad reflections.

The Duchess led her to the door into the card-room; then, after looking round the room as if in search of some one--"And there is Soulanges!" she said in deep tones.

The Countess shuddered as she saw, in the least brilliantly lighted corner, the pale, set face of Soulanges stretched in an easy-chair. The indifference of his attitude and the rigidity of his brow betrayed his suffering. The players passed him to and fro, without paying any more attention to him than if he had been dead. The picture of the wife in tears, and the dejected, morose husband, separated in the midst of this festivity like the two halves of a tree blasted by lightning, had perhaps a prophetic significance for the Countess. She dreaded lest she here saw an image of the revenges the future might have in store for her. Her heart was not yet so dried up that the feeling and generosity were entirely excluded, and she pressed the Duchess' hand, while thanking her by one of those smiles which have a certain childlike grace.

"My dear child," the old lady said in her ear, "remember henceforth that we are just as capable of repelling a man's attentions as of attracting them."

"She is yours if you are not a simpleton." These words were whispered into Colonel Montcornet's ear by Madame de Lansac, while the handsome Countess was still absorbed in compassion at the sight of Soulanges, for she still loved him truly enough to wish to restore him to happiness, and was promising herself in her own mind that she would exert the irresistible power her charms still had over him to make him return to his wife.

"Oh! I will talk to him!" said she to Madame de Lansac.

"Do nothing of the kind, my dear!" cried the old lady, as she went back to her armchair. "Choose a good husband, and shut your door to my nephew. Believe me, my child, a wife cannot accept her husband's heart as the gift of another woman; she is a hundred times happier in the belief that she has reconquered it. By bringing my niece here I believe I have given her an excellent chance of regaining her husband's affection. All the assistance I need of you is to play the Colonel." She pointed to the Baron's friend, and the Countess smiled.

"Well, madame, do you at last know the name of the unknown?" asked Martial, with an air of pique, to the Countess when he saw her alone.

"Yes," said Madame de Vaudremont, looking him in the face.

Her features expressed as much roguery as fun. The smile which gave life to her lips and cheeks, the liquid brightness of her eyes, were like the will-o'-the-wisp which leads travelers astray. Martial, who believed that she still loved him, assumed the coquetting graces in which a man is so ready to lull himself in the presence of the woman he loves. He said with a fatuous air:

"And will you be annoyed with me if I seem to attach great importance to your telling me that name?"

"Will you be annoyed with me," answered Madame de Vaudremont, "if a remnant of affection prevents my telling you; and if I forbid you to make the smallest advances to that young lady? It would be at the risk of your life perhaps."

"To lose your good graces, madame, would be worse than to lose my life."

"Martial," said the Countess severely, "she is Madame de Soulanges. Her husband would blow your brains out--if, indeed, you have any----"

"Ha! ha!" laughed the coxcomb. "What! the Colonel can leave the man in peace who has robbed him of your love, and then would fight for his wife! What a subversion of principles!--I beg of you to allow me to dance with the little lady. You will then be able to judge how little love that heart of ice could feel for you; for, if the Colonel disapproves of my dancing with his wife after allowing me to----"

"But she loves her husband."

"A still further obstacle that I shall have the pleasure of conquering."

"But she is married."

"A whimsical objection!"

"Ah!" said the Countess, with a bitter smile, "you punish us alike for our faults and our repentance!"

"Do not be angry!" exclaimed Martial eagerly. "Oh, forgive me, I beseech you. There, I will think no more of Madame de Soulanges."

"You deserve that I should send you to her."

"I am off then," said the Baron, laughing, "and I shall return more devoted to you than ever. You will see that the prettiest woman in the world cannot capture the heart that is yours."

"That is to say, that you want to win Colonel Montcornet's horse?"

"Ah! Traitor!" said he, threatening his friend with his finger. The Colonel smiled and joined them; the Baron gave him the seat near the Countess, saying to her with a sardonic accent:

"Here, madame, is a man who boasted that he could win your good graces in one evening."

He went away, thinking himself clever to have piqued the Countess' pride and done Montcornet an ill turn; but, in spite of his habitual keenness, he had not appreciated the irony underlying Madame de Vaudremont's speech, and did not perceive that she had come as far to meet his friend as his friend towards her, though both were unconscious of it.

At that moment when the lawyer went fluttering up to the candelabrum by which Madame de Soulanges sat, pale, timid, and apparently alive only in her eyes, her husband came to the door of the ballroom, his eyes flashing with anger. The old Duchess, watchful of everything, flew to her nephew, begged him to give her his arm and find her carriage, affecting to be mortally bored, and hoping thus to prevent a vexatious outbreak. Before going she fired a singular glance of intelligence at her niece, indicating the enterprising knight who was about to address her, and this signal seemed to say, "There he is, avenge yourself!"

Madame de Vaudremont caught these looks of the aunt and niece; a sudden light dawned on her mind; she was frightened lest she was the dupe of this old woman, so cunning and so practised in intrigue.

"That perfidious Duchess," said she to herself, "has perhaps been amusing herself by preaching morality to me while playing me some spiteful trick of her own."

At this thought Madame de Vaudremont's pride was perhaps more roused than her curiosity to disentangle the thread of this intrigue. In the absorption of mind to which she was a prey she was no longer mistress of herself. The Colonel, interpreting to his own advantage the embarrassment evident in the Countess' manner and speech, became more ardent and pressing. The old blasé diplomates, amusing themselves by watching the play of faces, had never found so many intrigues at once to watch or guess at. The passions agitating the two couples were to be seen with variations at every step in the crowded rooms, and reflected with different shades in other countenances. The spectacle of so many vivid passions, of all these lovers' quarrels, these pleasing revenges, these cruel favors, these flaming glances, of all this ardent life diffused around them, only made them feel their impotence more keenly.

At last the Baron had found a seat by Madame de Soulanges. His eyes stole a long look at her neck, as fresh as dew and as fragrant as field flowers. He admired close at hand the beauty which had amazed him from afar. He could see a small, well-shod foot, and measure with his eye a slender and graceful shape. At that time women wore their sash tied close under the bosom, in imitation of Greek statues, a pitiless fashion for those whose bust was faulty. As he cast furtive glances at the Countess' figure, Martial was enchanted with its perfection.

"You have not danced once this evening, madame," said he in soft and flattering tones. "Not, I should suppose, for lack of a partner?"

"I never go to parties; I am quite unknown," replied Madame de Soulanges coldly, not having understood the look by which her aunt had just conveyed to her that she was to attract the Baron.

Martial, to give himself countenance, twisted the diamond he wore on his left hand; the rainbow fires of the gem seemed to flash a sudden light on the young Countess' mind; she blushed and looked at the Baron with an undefinable expression.

"Do you like dancing?" asked the Provencal, to reopen the conversation.

"Yes, very much, monsieur."

At this strange reply their eyes met. The young man, surprised by the earnest accent, which aroused a vague hope in his heart, had suddenly questioned the lady's eyes.

"Then, madame, am I not overbold in offering myself to be your partner for the next quadrille?"

Artless confusion colored the Countess' white cheeks.

"But, monsieur, I have already refused one partner--a military man----"

"Was it that tall cavalry colonel whom you see over there?"

"Precisely so."

"Oh! he is a friend of mine; feel no alarm. Will you grant me the favor I dare hope for?"

"Yes, monsieur."

Her tone betrayed an emotion so new and so deep that the lawyer's world-worn soul was touched. He was overcome by shyness like a schoolboy's, lost his confidence, and his southern brain caught fire; he tried to talk, but his phrases struck him as graceless in comparison with Madame de Soulanges' bright and subtle replies. It was lucky for him that the quadrille was forming. Standing by his beautiful partner, he felt more at ease. To many men dancing is a phase of being; they think that they can more powerfully influence the heart of woman by displaying the graces of their bodies than by their intellect. Martial wished, no doubt, at this moment to put forth all his most effective seductions, to judge by the pretentiousness of his movements and gestures.

He led his conquest to the quadrille in which the most brilliant women in the room made it a point of chimerical importance to dance in preference to any other. While the orchestra played the introductory bars to the first figure, the Baron felt it an incredible gratification to his pride to perceive, as he reviewed the ladies forming the lines of that formidable square, that Madame de Soulanges' dress might challenge that even of Madame de Vaudremont, who, by a chance not perhaps unsought, was standing with Montcornet /vis-a-vis/ to himself and the lady in blue. All eyes were for a moment turned on Madame de Soulanges; a flattering murmur showed that she was the subject of every man's conversation with his partner. Looks of admiration and envy centered on her, with so much eagerness that the young creature, abashed by a triumph she seemed to disclaim, modestly looked down, blushed, and was all the more charming. When she raised her white eyelids it was to look at her ravished partner as though she wished to transfer the glory of this admiration to him, and to say that she cared more for his than for all the rest. She threw her innocence into her vanity; or rather she seemed to give herself up to the guileless admiration which is the beginning of love, with the good faith found only in youthful hearts. As she danced, the lookers-on might easily believe that she displayed her grace for Martial alone; and though she was modest, and new to the trickery of the ballroom, she knew as well as the most accomplished coquette how to raise her eyes to his at the right moment and drop their lids with assumed modesty.

When the movement of a new figure, invented by a dancer named Trenis, and named after him, brought Martial face to face with the Colonel--"I have won your horse," said he, laughing.

"Yes, but you have lost eighty thousand francs a year!" retorted Montcornet, glancing at Madame de Vaudremont.

"What do I care?" replied Martial. "Madame de Soulanges is worth millions!"

At the end of the quadrille more than one whisper was poured into more than one ear. The less pretty women made moral speeches to their partners, commenting on the budding liaison between Martial and the Comtesse de Soulanges. The handsomest wondered at her easy surrender. The men could not understand such luck as the Baron's, not regarding him as particularly fascinating. A few indulgent women said it was not fair to judge the Countess too hastily; young wives would be in a very hapless plight if an expressive look or a few graceful dancing steps were enough to compromise a woman.

Martial alone knew the extent of his happiness. During the last figure, when the ladies had to form the /moulinet/, his fingers clasped those of the Countess, and he fancied that, through the thin perfumed kid of her gloves, the young wife's grasp responded to his amorous appeal.

"Madame," said he, as the quadrille ended, "do not go back to the odious corner where you have been burying your face and your dress until now. Is admiration the only benefit you can obtain from the jewels that adorn your white neck and beautifully dressed hair? Come and take a turn through the rooms to enjoy the scene and yourself."

Madame de Soulanges yielded to her seducer, who thought she would be his all the more surely if he could only show her off. Side by side they walked two or three times amid the groups who crowded the rooms. The Comtesse de Soulanges, evidently uneasy, paused for an instant at each door before entering, only doing so after stretching her neck to look at all the men there. This alarm, which crowned the Baron's satisfaction, did not seem to be removed till he said to her, "Make yourself easy; /he/ is not here."

They thus made their way to an immense picture gallery in a wing of the mansion, where their eyes could feast in anticipation on the splendid display of a collation prepared for three hundred persons. As supper was about to begin, Martial led the Countess to an oval boudoir looking on to the garden, where the rarest flowers and a few shrubs made a scented bower under bright blue hangings. The murmurs of the festivity here died away. The Countess, at first startled, refused firmly to follow the young man; but, glancing in a mirror, she no doubt assured herself that they could be seen, for she seated herself on an ottoman with a fairly good grace.

"This room is charming," said she, admiring the sky-blue hangings looped with pearls.

"All here is love and delight!" said the Baron, with deep emotion.

In the mysterious light which prevailed he looked at the Countess, and detected on her gently agitated face an expression of uneasiness, modesty, and eagerness which enchanted him. The young lady smiled, and this smile seemed to put an end to the struggle of feeling surging in her heart; in the most insinuating way she took her adorer's left hand, and drew from his finger the ring on which she had fixed her eyes.

"What a fine diamond!" she exclaimed in the artless tone of a young girl betraying the incitement of a first temptation.

Martial, troubled by the Countess' involuntary but intoxicating touch, like a caress, as she drew off the ring, looked at her with eyes as glittering as the gem.

"Wear it," he said, "in memory of this hour, and for the love of----"

She was looking at him with such rapture that he did not end the sentence; he kissed her hand.

"You give it me?" she said, looking much astonished.

"I wish I had the whole world to offer you!"

"You are not joking?" she went on, in a voice husky with too great satisfaction.

"Will you accept only my diamond?"

"You will never take it back?" she insisted.

"Never."

She put the ring on her finger. Martial, confident of coming happiness, was about to put his hand round her waist, but she suddenly rose, and said in a clear voice, without any agitation:

"I accept the diamond, monsieur, with the less scruple because it belongs to me."

The Baron was speechless.

"Monsieur de Soulanges took it lately from my dressing-table, and told me he had lost it."

"You are mistaken, madame," said Martial, nettled. "It was given me by Madame de Vaudremont."

"Precisely so," she said with a smile. "My husband borrowed this ring of me, he gave it to her, she made it a present to you; my ring has made a little journey, that is all. This ring will perhaps tell me all I do not know, and teach me the secret of always pleasing.--Monsieur," she went on, "if it had not been my own, you may be sure I should not have risked paying so dear for it; for a young woman, it is said, is in danger with you. But, you see," and she touched a spring within the ring, "here is M. de Soulanges' hair."

She fled into the crowded rooms so swiftly, that it seemed useless to try to follow her; besides, Martial, utterly confounded, was in no mood to carry the adventure further. The Countess' laugh found an echo in the boudoir, where the young coxcomb now perceived, between two shrubs, the Colonel and Madame de Vaudremont, both laughing heartily.

"Will you have my horse, to ride after your prize?" said the Colonel.

The Baron took the banter poured upon him by Madame de Vaudremont and Montcornet with a good grace, which secured their silence as to the events of the evening, when his friend exchanged his charger for a rich and pretty young wife.

As the Comtesse de Soulanges drove across Paris from the Chausee d'Antin to the Faubourg Saint-Germain, where she lived, her soul was prey to many alarms. Before leaving the Hotel Gondreville she went through all the rooms, but found neither her aunt nor her husband, who had gone away without her. Frightful suspicions then tortured her ingenuous mind. A silent witness of her husbands' torments since the day when Madame de Vaudremont had chained him to her car, she had confidently hoped that repentance would ere long restore her husband to her. It was with unspeakable repugnance that she had consented to the scheme plotted by her aunt, Madame de Lansac, and at this moment she feared she had made a mistake.

The evening's experience had saddened her innocent soul. Alarmed at first by the Count's look of suffering and dejection, she had become more so on seeing her rival's beauty, and the corruption of society had gripped her heart. As she crossed the Pont Royal she threw away the desecrated hair at the back of the diamond, given to her once as a token of the purest affection. She wept as she remembered the bitter grief to which she had so long been a victim, and shuddered more than once as she reflected that the duty of a woman, who wishes for peace in her home, compels her to bury sufferings so keen as hers at the bottom of her heart, and without a complaint.

"Alas!" thought she, "what can women do when they do not love? What is the fount of their indulgence? I cannot believe that, as my aunt tells me, reason is all-sufficient to maintain them in such devotion."

She was still sighing when her man-servant let down the handsome carriage-step down which she flew into the hall of her house. She rushed precipitately upstairs, and when she reached her room was startled by seeing her husband sitting by the fire.

"How long is it, my dear, since you have gone to balls without telling me beforehand?" he asked in a broken voice. "You must know that a woman is always out of place without her husband. You compromised yourself strangely by remaining in the dark corner where you had ensconced yourself."

"Oh, my dear, good Leon," said she in a coaxing tone, "I could not resist the happiness of seeing you without your seeing me. My aunt took me to this ball, and I was very happy there!"

This speech disarmed the Count's looks of their assumed severity, for he had been blaming himself while dreading his wife's return, no doubt fully informed at the ball of an infidelity he had hoped to hide from her; and, as is the way of lovers conscious of their guilt, he tried, by being the first to find fault, to escape her just anger. Happy in seeing her husband smile, and in finding him at this hour in a room whither of late he had come more rarely, the Countess looked at him so tenderly that she blushed and cast down her eyes. Her clemency enraptured Soulanges all the more, because this scene followed on the misery he had endured at the ball. He seized his wife's hand and kissed it gratefully. Is not gratitude often a part of love?

"Hortense, what is that on your finger that has hurt my lip so much?" asked he, laughing.

"It is my diamond which you said you had lost, and which I have found."

General Montcornet did not marry Madame de Vaudremont, in spite of the mutual understanding in which they had lived for a few minutes, for she was one of the victims of the terrible fire which sealed the fame of the ball given by the Austrian ambassador on the occasion of Napoleon's marriage with the daughter of the Emperor Joseph II.

JULY, 1829.

The Codes Of Hammurabi And Moses
W. W. Davies

QTY

The discovery of the Hammurabi Code is one of the greatest achievements of archaeology, and is of paramount interest, not only to the student of the Bible, but also to all those interested in ancient history...

Religion   ISBN: *1-59462-338-4*   **Pages:132**
MSRP $12.95

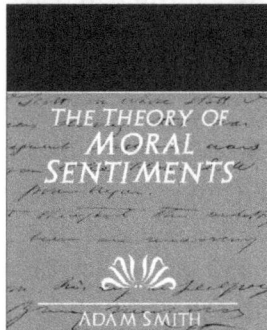

The Theory of Moral Sentiments
Adam Smith

QTY

This work from 1749. contains original theories of conscience amd moral judgment and it is the foundation for systemof morals.

Philosophy ISBN: *1-59462-777-0*   **Pages:536**
MSRP $19.95

Jessica's First Prayer
Hesba Stretton

QTY

In a screened and secluded corner of one of the many railway-bridges which span the streets of London there could be seen a few years ago, from five o'clock every morning until half past eight, a tidily set-out coffee-stall, consisting of a trestle and board, upon which stood two large tin cans, with a small fire of charcoal burning under each so as to keep the coffee boiling during the early hours of the morning when the work-people were thronging into the city on their way to their daily toil...

Pages:84

Childrens   ISBN: *1-59462-373-2*   *MSRP $9.95*

My Life and Work
Henry Ford

QTY

Henry Ford revolutionized the world with his implementation of mass production for the Model T automobile. Gain valuable business insight into his life and work with his own auto-biography... "We have only started on our development of our country we have not as yet, with all our talk of wonderful progress, done more than scratch the surface. The progress has been wonderful enough but..."

Pages:300

Biographies/   ISBN: *1-59462-198-5*   *MSRP $21.95*

The Art of Cross-Examination
Francis Wellman

QTY

I presume it is the experience of every author, after his first book is published upon an important subject, to be almost overwhelmed with a wealth of ideas and illustrations which could readily have been included in his book, and which to his own mind, at least, seem to make a second edition inevitable. Such certainly was the case with me; and when the first edition had reached its sixth impression in five months, I rejoiced to learn that it seemed to my publishers that the book had met with a sufficiently favorable reception to justify a second and considerably enlarged edition. ..

Pages:412

Reference   ISBN: *1-59462-647-2*   *MSRP $19.95*

On the Duty of Civil Disobedience
Henry David Thoreau

QTY

Thoreau wrote his famous essay, On the Duty of Civil Disobedience, as a protest against an unjust but popular war and the immoral but popular institution of slave-owning. He did more than write—he declined to pay his taxes, and was hauled off to gaol in consequence. Who can say how much this refusal of his hastened the end of the war and of slavery ?

Law   ISBN: *1-59462-747-9*

Pages:48

MSRP $7.45

Dream Psychology Psychoanalysis for Beginners
Sigmund Freud

QTY

Sigmund Freud, born Sigismund Schlomo Freud (May 6, 1856 - September 23, 1939), was a Jewish-Austrian neurologist and psychiatrist who co-founded the psychoanalytic school of psychology. Freud is best known for his theories of the unconscious mind, especially involving the mechanism of repression; his redefinition of sexual desire as mobile and directed towards a wide variety of objects; and his therapeutic techniques, especially his understanding of transference in the therapeutic relationship and the presumed value of dreams as sources of insight into unconscious desires.

Pages:196

Psychology   ISBN: *1-59462-905-6*   *MSRP $15.45*

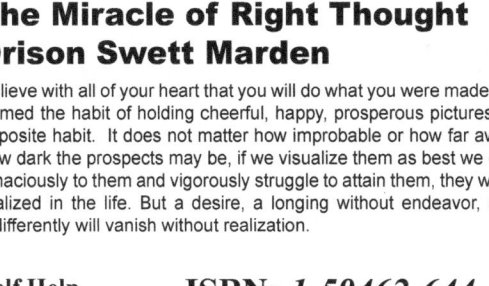

The Miracle of Right Thought
Orison Swett Marden

QTY

Believe with all of your heart that you will do what you were made to do. When the mind has once formed the habit of holding cheerful, happy, prosperous pictures, it will not be easy to form the opposite habit. It does not matter how improbable or how far away this realization may see, or how dark the prospects may be, if we visualize them as best we can, as vividly as possible, hold tenaciously to them and vigorously struggle to attain them, they will gradually become actualized, realized in the life. But a desire, a longing without endeavor, a yearning abandoned or held indifferently will vanish without realization.

Pages:360

Self Help   ISBN: *1-59462-644-8*   *MSRP $25.45*

The Rosicrucian Cosmo-Conception Mystic Christianity *by Max Heindel*　ISBN: *1-59462-188-8*　**$38.95**
The Rosicrucian Cosmo-conception is not dogmatic, neither does it appeal to any other authority than the reason of the student. It is: not controversial, but is: sent forth in the, hope that it may help to clear...　New Age/Religion Pages 646

Abandonment To Divine Providence *by Jean-Pierre de Caussade*　ISBN: *1-59462-228-0*　**$25.95**
"The Rev. Jean Pierre de Caussade was one of the most remarkable spiritual writers of the Society of Jesus in France in the 18th Century. His death took place at Toulouse in 1751. His works have gone through many editions and have been republished...　Inspirational/Religion Pages 400

Mental Chemistry *by Charles Haanel*　ISBN: *1-59462-192-6*　**$23.95**
Mental Chemistry allows the change of material conditions by combining and appropriately utilizing the power of the mind. Much like applied chemistry creates something new and unique out of careful combinations of chemicals the mastery of mental chemistry...　New Age Pages 354

The Letters of Robert Browning and Elizabeth Barret Barrett 1845-1846 vol II　ISBN: *1-59462-193-4*　**$35.95**
by Robert Browning and Elizabeth Barrett　Biographies Pages 596

Gleanings In Genesis (volume I) *by Arthur W. Pink*　ISBN: *1-59462-130-6*　**$27.45**
Appropriately has Genesis been termed "the seed plot of the Bible" for in it we have, in germ form, almost all of the great doctrines which are afterwards fully developed in the books of Scripture which follow...　Religion/Inspirational Pages 420

The Master Key *by L. W. de Laurence*　ISBN: *1-59462-001-6*　**$30.95**
In no branch of human knowledge has there been a more lively increase of the spirit of research during the past few years than in the study of Psychology, Concentration and Mental Discipline. The requests for authentic lessons in Thought Control, Mental Discipline and...　New Age/Business Pages 422

The Lesser Key Of Solomon Goetia *by L. W. de Laurence*　ISBN: *1-59462-092-X*　**$9.95**
This translation of the first book of the "Lernegton" which is now for the first time made accessible to students of Talismanic Magic was done, after careful collation and edition, from numerous Ancient Manuscripts in Hebrew, Latin, and French...　New Age/Occult Pages 92

Rubaiyat Of Omar Khayyam *by Edward Fitzgerald*　ISBN:*1-59462-332-5*　**$13.95**
Edward Fitzgerald, whom the world has already learned, in spite of his own efforts to remain within the shadow of anonymity, to look upon as one of the rarest poets of the century, was born at Bredfield, in Suffolk, on the 31st of March, 1809. He was the third son of John Purcell...　Music Pages 172

Ancient Law *by Henry Maine*　ISBN: *1-59462-128-4*　**$29.95**
The chief object of the following pages is to indicate some of the earliest ideas of mankind, as they are reflected in Ancient Law, and to point out the relation of those ideas to modern thought.　Religion/History Pages 452

Far-Away Stories *by William J. Locke*　ISBN: *1-59462-129-2*　**$19.45**
"Good wine needs no bush, but a collection of mixed vintages does. And this book is just such a collection. Some of the stories I do not want to remain buried for ever in the museum files of dead magazine-numbers an author's not unpardonable vanity..."　Fiction Pages 272

Life of David Crockett *by David Crockett*　ISBN: *1-59462-250-7*　**$27.45**
"Colonel David Crockett was one of the most remarkable men of the times in which he lived. Born in humble life, but gifted with a strong will, an indomitable courage, and unremitting perseverance...　Biographies/New Age Pages 424

Lip-Reading *by Edward Nitchie*　ISBN: *1-59462-206-X*　**$25.95**
Edward B. Nitchie, founder of the New York School for the Hard of Hearing, now the Nitchie School of Lip-Reading, Inc, wrote "LIP-READING Principles and Practice". The development and perfecting of this meritorious work on lip-reading was an undertaking...　How-to Pages 400

A Handbook of Suggestive Therapeutics, Applied Hypnotism, Psychic Science　ISBN: *1-59462-214-0*　**$24.95**
by Henry Munro　Health/New Age/Health/Self-help Pages 376

A Doll's House: and Two Other Plays *by Henrik Ibsen*　ISBN: *1-59462-112-8*　**$19.95**
Henrik Ibsen created this classic when in revolutionary 1848 Rome. Introducing some striking concepts in playwriting for the realist genre, this play has been studied the world over.　Fiction/Classics/Plays 308

The Light of Asia *by sir Edwin Arnold*　ISBN: *1-59462-204-3*　**$13.95**
In this poetic masterpiece, Edwin Arnold describes the life and teachings of Buddha. The man who was to become known as Buddha to the world was born as Prince Gautama of India but he rejected the worldly riches and abandoned the reigns of power when...　Religion/History/Biographies Pages 170

The Complete Works of Guy de Maupassant *by Guy de Maupassant*　ISBN: *1-59462-157-8*　**$16.95**
"For days and days, nights and nights, I had dreamed of that first kiss which was to consecrate our engagement, and I knew not on what spot I should put my lips..."　Fiction/Classics Pages 240

The Art of Cross-Examination *by Francis L. Wellman*　ISBN: *1-59462-309-0*　**$26.95**
Written by a renowned trial lawyer, Wellman imparts his experience and uses case studies to explain how to use psychology to extract desired information through questioning.　How-to/Science/Reference Pages 408

Answered or Unanswered? *by Louisa Vaughan*　ISBN: *1-59462-248-5*　**$10.95**
Miracles of Faith in China　Religion Pages 112

The Edinburgh Lectures on Mental Science (1909) *by Thomas*　ISBN: *1-59462-008-3*　**$11.95**
This book contains the substance of a course of lectures recently given by the writer in the Queen Street Hall, Edinburgh. Its purpose is to indicate the Natural Principles governing the relation between Mental Action and Material Conditions...　New Age/Psychology Pages 148

Ayesha *by H. Rider Haggard*　ISBN: *1-59462-301-5*　**$24.95**
Verily and indeed it is the unexpected that happens! Probably if there was one person upon the earth from whom the Editor of this, and of a certain previous history, did not expect to hear again...　Classics Pages 380

Ayala's Angel *by Anthony Trollope*　ISBN: *1-59462-352-X*　**$29.95**
The two girls were both pretty, but Lucy who was twenty-one who supposed to be simple and comparatively unattractive, whereas Ayala was credited, as her Bombwhat romantic name might show, with poetic charm and a taste for romance. Ayala when her father died was nineteen...　Fiction Pages 484

The American Commonwealth *by James Bryce*　ISBN: *1-59462-286-8*　**$34.45**
An interpretation of American democratic political theory. It examines political mechanics and society from the perspective of Scotsman James Bryce　Politics Pages 572

Stories of the Pilgrims *by Margaret P. Pumphrey*　ISBN: *1-59462-116-0*　**$17.95**
This book explores pilgrims religious oppression in England as well as their escape to Holland and eventual crossing to America on the Mayflower, and their early days in New England...　History Pages 268

QTY

The Fasting Cure *by Sinclair Upton*   ISBN: *1-59462-222-1* **$13.95**
In the Cosmopolitan Magazine for May, 1910, and in the Contemporary Review (London) for April, 1910, I published an article dealing with my experiences in fasting. I have written a great many magazine articles, but never one which attracted so much attention... New Age/Self Help/Health Pages 164

Hebrew Astrology *by Sepharial*   ISBN: *1-59462-308-2* **$13.45**
In these days of advanced thinking it is a matter of common observation that we have left many of the old landmarks behind and that we are now pressing forward to greater heights and to a wider horizon than that which represented the mind-content of our progenitors... Astrology Pages 144

Thought Vibration or The Law of Attraction in the Thought World   ISBN: *1-59462-127-6* **$12.95**

by William Walker Atkinson   *Psychology/Religion Pages 144*

Optimism *by Helen Keller*   ISBN: *1-59462-108-X* **$15.95**
Helen Keller was blind, deaf, and mute since 19 months old, yet famously learned how to overcome these handicaps, communicate with the world, and spread her lectures promoting optimism. An inspiring read for everyone... Biographies/Inspirational Pages 84

Sara Crewe *by Frances Burnett*   ISBN: *1-59462-360-0* **$9.45**
In the first place, Miss Minchin lived in London. Her home was a large, dull, tall one, in a large, dull square, where all the houses were alike, and all the sparrows were alike, and where all the door-knockers made the same heavy sound... Childrens/Classic Pages 88

The Autobiography of Benjamin Franklin *by Benjamin Franklin*   ISBN: *1-59462-135-7* **$24.95**
The Autobiography of Benjamin Franklin has probably been more extensively read than any other American historical work, and no other book of its kind has had such ups and downs of fortune. Franklin lived for many years in England, where he was agent... Biographies/History Pages 332

Name	
Email	
Telephone	
Address	
City, State ZIP	

☐ **Credit Card**   ☐ **Check / Money Order**

Credit Card Number	
Expiration Date	
Signature	

Please Mail to: Book Jungle
PO Box 2226
Champaign, IL 61825
or Fax to: 630-214-0564

ORDERING INFORMATION

web: *www.bookjungle.com*
email: *sales@bookjungle.com*
fax: *630-214-0564*
mail: *Book Jungle PO Box 2226 Champaign, IL 61825*
or PayPal *to sales@bookjungle.com*

Please contact us for bulk discounts

DIRECT-ORDER TERMS

**20% Discount if You Order
Two or More Books**
Free Domestic Shipping!
Accepted: Master Card, Visa,
Discover, American Express

www.ingramcontent.com/pod-product-compliance
Lightning Source LLC
Chambersburg PA
CBHW080749250626
47162CB00010B/3074